Think Again!

Written by Geraldine McCaughrean
Illustrated by Bee Willey

Collins

1 "This will never do!"

When Maker made the animals, he made a few mistakes. Everyone makes mistakes.

For instance, First Squirrel was as big as a bull.

First Autumn came along, and Squirrel began to gather food for the winter. She took melons and pumpkins and coconuts. She took breadfruit and marrows.

In fact, she stripped the fields and woods quite bare.

And when Squirrel looked for somewhere to store the food, there was no tree big enough to hold her winter larder.

"This will never do!" said Maker. "You'll leave nothing for my other animals to eat! I shall have to think again about you."

So he tapped Squirrel on the back, and down she shrank, to a squirrel-ish sort of size.

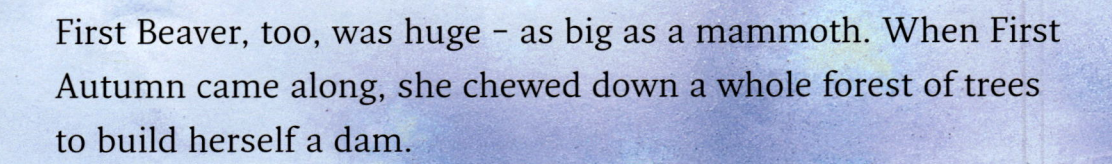

First Beaver, too, was huge – as big as a mammoth. When First Autumn came along, she chewed down a whole forest of trees to build herself a dam.

And that dam was so big that it choked three rivers, and the rivers all spilled over.

Floodwater covered the land from west to east and from north to south. It washed Squirrel's winter larder out of its hiding place and wetted Maker's feet.

"This will never do!" said Maker. "You and your dams will drown all the other animals I have made! I shall have to think again about you!"

So he tapped Beaver on the back, and down she shrank, to a beaver-ish sort of size.

Then there was Ant. Well, she was not so much "Ant" as **gi-ant**, with eyes like golf balls and jaws like a digger.

There was not a log of wood or prickly cactus anywhere on Earth that did not crumple flat under her.

"This will never do!" said Maker. "You would build ant hills taller than my mountains. Also, you would frighten the squeal out of Pig and the pips out of the pomegranates! You even frighten me! I shall have to think again about you!"

So he shrank the ant down to an ant-ish sort of size, which pleased her because she and her friends were party animals and liked to go about in a mob.

11

2 Moose and Mouse

As for Moose!
First Moose was so big that his antlers scraped the stars off the sky. His feet flattened hills. His bite tore up whole fields of corn and his breath was like a hurricane. When he bellowed, Beaver's dam collapsed.
In fact First Moose was positively **enor-moose!**

"This will never do!" said Maker. "If I let you loose in my world you'll ruin everything, with your stamping and your scraping and your bellowing and your trampling!"

So he tapped Moose on the back, and down Moose shrank, small as a mouse.

A mouse and a moose the same size? Impossible! Ridiculous! Think of the cats! They would never know which one to chase: the mouse or the moose! Think how silly the hunters would look, tracking mice through the undergrowth.

So Maker thought again, and made Moose a moose-ish sort of size. And after that everyone was happy ...

... except for Maker. Day after day, he kept hearing music – a high, soft, piping music. But look as he might, he could not see where it came from or who was making it.

3 "Show yourself!"

Maker sent Squirrel to look among the treetops, but the piping wasn't coming from the trees.

He sent Beaver to look underwater, but the piping wasn't coming from the rivers. He sent Ant to look under the stones and the rocks, but the piping wasn't there. Nor was it underground among the worms and the daisy roots.

He sent Moose deep into the forests to look, but Moose was rather short-sighted. He only bumped into trees and got his antlers caught in the branches.

Still the music came fluting and peeping past Maker's ear. "Show yourself!" shouted Maker at last. "Come out and show yourself, whoever you are!"

First Elephant peeped out from behind a blade of grass. "I was just blowing my nose!" he squeaked. "I caught a cold when Enor-Moose was doing all that bellowing and snorting. I'm sorry if I disturbed you."

"This won't do! This won't do at all!" said Maker. "You're so small that anyone might tread on you – and *then* what would become of your wonderful music?"

So he tapped Elephant on his tiny back.

First Elephant grew as big as an ant ... as big as a mouse ... as big as a squirrel ... as big as a beaver and bigger ...

He grew as big as a moose and still he went on growing – especially his ears.

"Now blow," said Maker, looking up at Enormous Elephant.

So Elephant blew his nose, and out came a noise like five hundred brass bands.

Elephant winced. "Sorry. I think I blew too hard."

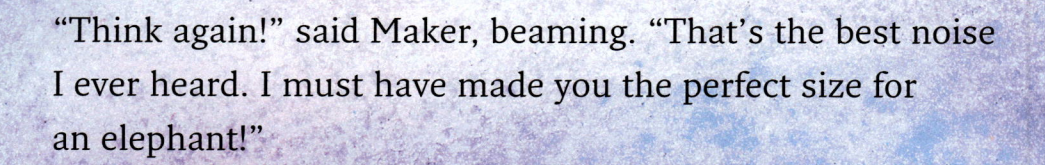

"Think again!" said Maker, beaming. "That's the best noise I ever heard. I must have made you the perfect size for an elephant!"

After that, he turned to Whale, who (in those days) was about as big as a tadpole. "If I make you bigger," he said, "will you sing for me too, and fill the oceans with song?"

"Oh yes!" said Whale. "If you will make me big!"

So that is why the Whale is so huge, and why, now and then, her mysterious, whistling song carries over the sea, making the waves shiver with joy.

Word spread to the Birds, who (in those days) were as big as pigs and lions and hippopotamuses, and made a terrible racket with their grunting and growling and roaring and snuffling.
"Can we sing for you too?" they said.
"I suppose so," said Maker doubtfully. "But I will have to make you smaller."

"Oh, no, no," grunted the Birds, pecking their pick-axe beaks deep into the ground. "We don't want to be smaller. Cat would only pick on us. You know how unkind Life is to the smallest creatures."

4 "What will you give us?"

Maker tried to think. (It was hard, because of all the noise the Birds were making.) "What if I were to give you a lovely present?" he said, teasing and tempting.

"What? What will you give us?" demanded the Birds in their big, booming voices.

Maker looked around him. The woods were already full of moose. The fields were full of mice. The earth was full of ants. The trees were full of squirrels. And everything was just about perfect, except … Turning his face to the sky, he felt the sun warm on his cheek.

"If you let me make you smaller, and if you will sing for me, I shall … I shall …"

"Yes? Yes?" screamed the Birds.

"I shall give you wings."

"Oh!" shrieked the Birds. "For wings we would do *anything!*"

So that is why birdsong is sweeter (and smaller) than it used to be, and why the morning skies are sometimes so full of birdsong that the whole world shivers with joy.

Oh, and don't worry about First Cat. Maker wove hedgerows for the birds to hide in, with thorns and brambles to keep out soft and prying paws.

The Maker thinks again

Before

whale   elephant   bird   squirrel   beaver

After

whale   elephant

ant		moose

moose		beaver		squirrel		bird		ant

31

Ideas for guided reading

Learning objectives: use knowledge to work out and check meanings of unfamiliar words; retell known stories, comparing oral stories with text; read aloud with intonation and expression appropriate to grammar and punctuation; present stories for the class.

Curriculum links: Citizenship: Choices; Science: Plants and Animals in the Local Environment, variation

Interest words: Maker, squirrel, pumpkins, coconuts, breadfruit, larder, mammoth, dam, hurricane, moose, beaver, piping, elephant, bellowing, squirrel, tadpole, birdsong

Word count: 1,136

Resources: tape or digital recorder

Getting started

This book may be read over two guided reading sessions.

- Show the children the front cover and discuss what is unusual about the picture (it shows a tiny elephant lost in the grass). Ask them to guess what the story is about, then read the blurb – were they right?
- Establish that this is a story similar to those from many cultures around the world which try to explain how the world was created.
- Skim through the pages with the children and ask what is happening in the story. Who is the Maker? Where is this story likely to have taken place? Is it a true story or not?

Reading and responding

- Before reading, discuss strategies for tackling unfamiliar words.
- Ask the children to read quietly and independently to the end of p15. Ask each child to read aloud a short passage, prompting and praising their use of strategies.
- Ask them to retell in their own words what has happened so far, and then predict what may happen in the second half of the story. Ask them to continue to read independently to p29.